D1550586

Old Mahony and the Bear Family

Old Mahony and the Bear Family

By Wolfram Hänel
Pictures by Jean-Pierre Corderoc'h

Translated by
Rosemary Lanning

North-South Books

NEW YORK · LONDON

Copyright © 1997 by Nord-Süd Verlag AG, Gossau Zürich, Switzerland
First published in Switzerland under the title *Eine Falle für Familie Bär.*
English translation copyright © 1997 by North-South Books Inc.

First published in the United States, Great Britain, Canada,
Australia, and New Zealand in 1997 by North-South Books,
an imprint of Nord-Süd Verlag AG, Gossau Zürich, Switzerland.

Distributed in the United States by North-South Books Inc., New York.

Library of Congress Cataloging-in-Publication Data is available.
A CIP catalogue record for this book is available from The British Library.
ISBN 1-55858-713-6 (trade binding)
1 3 5 7 9 TB 10 8 6 4 2
ISBN 1-55858-714-4 (library binding)
1 3 5 7 9 LB 10 8 6 4 2
Printed in Belgium

For more information about our books, and the authors and artists
who create them, visit our web site: http://www.northsouth.com

It was summer. The sun was shining.
Old Mahony and Big Bill stood in the
middle of the river. Each was fishing in
his own way—the old man with his
fishing rod, and the bear with his huge
paws. They were the best of friends.

A butterfly flitted overhead. Old Mahony whistled happily to himself. And Big Bill growled contentedly. Life was grand.

Just as Old Mahony hooked another fat fish, Big Bill suddenly lifted his nose high and sniffed the air. Then he waded over to the bank.

"Where's he going?" Old Mahony wondered, pulling his fish out of the water. The salmon gleamed in the sunshine.

8

"One more of you little fellows," said
the old man, "and I'll have enough for
my breakfast tomorrow." He cast his
line again.

The water gurgled gently around Old Mahony's rubber boots. Suddenly there was a splish and a splash behind him.

"Big Bill must be back," Old Mahony muttered, turning his head. He almost dropped the fishing rod, for there stood a strange bear! Much, much bigger than Big Bill! And he looked scary!

The strange bear reached into Old Mahony's bag, pulled out one of the salmon—and ate it up! Just one bite, and the fish disappeared.

"Hold on a minute," yelled Old Mahony. "You can't do that!"

The strange bear burped and waded farther out into the river. The old man looked around, not knowing what to do. Just then he spotted Big Bill disappearing between the trees on the bank.

"Well, blow me down!" exclaimed Old Mahony. "What's going on?"

The strange bear had moved downstream where the water was too deep for Old Mahony, who could only watch as the bear took one fish after another out of the river.

The bear gobbled them down as if he
hadn't eaten for days.

"All right," growled Old Mahony. "You
eat your fill, old chap. There will still be
enough for both of us."

He was just about to cast his line again
when . . .

"What's that?" he whispered. "I must be
dreaming."

There, where the flat rocks reached far
out into the river, two bear cubs were
splashing around.

They moved quite awkwardly, with
paws that seemed much too big for their
bodies. Near them sat the mother bear,
keeping watch.

Then Big Bill came back out of the
forest.

But Big Bill was not alone! He was leading a very old bear, whose fur was quite gray.

"I don't believe it," groaned Old Mahony. "It is a whole family."

The bear cubs were learning to dive.
Even the grandfather was rolling around
in the water, snorting with pleasure. The
water eddied and foamed, and all the fish
were scared off.

Big Bill showed the bear cubs how to make the best splashes. Splosh! Old Mahony got a faceful of water.

Old Mahony was fed up.

He stood in front of the bear family and shouted: "BOO!"

But the bears just went on paddling and splashing. Big Bill was behaving worst of all.

"That's enough!" yelled Old Mahony.

"Get out of here! Scram! This is my river!" he shouted. Splosh! Another blast of water hit him right in the face. It ran over his hair, into his ears, and down the back of his shirt.

The old man picked up his fishing rod and waded to the bank.

That night he sat in front of his cabin eating beans for supper. His mood had not improved, not one little bit.

But then he had an idea. . . .

The next morning the old man went to the shed and rummaged around until he found an old spade and a pickaxe.

He plodded across the meadow, almost as far as the river, and started digging. He dug and dug until the hole was so deep that only his head could be seen. Then he climbed out of the hole, got a ladder, stood the ladder in the hole, and went on digging.

By evening the pit was almost as deep as the ladder was tall. The old man nodded in satisfaction. Then he climbed out and pulled up the ladder. But he wasn't finished yet. He got a few branches and some twigs, and laid them across the pit. Then he carefully covered them with grass, so that the trap was almost impossible to see.

The sun was setting. The bears vanished into the forest, each with a fat fish between its teeth.

"Just you wait," growled Old Mahony. "The fun's soon going to be over for you."

The next morning he would lure the bears across the river . . .

Right into the pit.

Old Mahony rubbed his hands together and chuckled.

One more night, then the river will
belong to me again, thought Old Mahony.
I don't mind if Big Bill stays, but the rest
of them have got to go!

I'll sell them to a zoo. Or a circus. Then
I'll be rid of them for good, and I'll finally
be able to fish in peace again!

Old Mahony yawned.

Time for bed, he thought, and headed for his cabin. But by then it was so dark that he could hardly see.

"Drat!" he said, and felt his way
carefully to the left. Wait! The pit must
be somewhere around here. Better to go
right a bit. One step. Another step . . .

Something cracked and snapped under
Old Mahony. He tottered and waved his
arms around wildly. Then a branch broke,
and Old Mahony tumbled down. Way,
way down.

"Help!" cried Old Mahony. He stood
in the pit, groaning.

It was cold and damp. The old man was shivering. And hungry. His stomach rumbled like a pack of wild dogs. His left arm hurt, and he was scared, too. How was he going to get out of the pit?

At last he fell asleep.

He tossed and turned, dreaming strange dreams. The bears had sold *him* to a circus where he had to dance every night. With a ring through his nose!

Old Mahony woke with a start. He felt stiff and even more hungry and he still didn't know how to get out of the pit. Suddenly he heard footsteps. *Heavy* footsteps. Chunks of earth and tufts of grass came rattling down on him.

Then, high above him, he saw Big Bill's face! The bear carefully edged over to the pit and stretched out his paw to the old man. But however hard he tried, Old Mahony couldn't reach the paw.

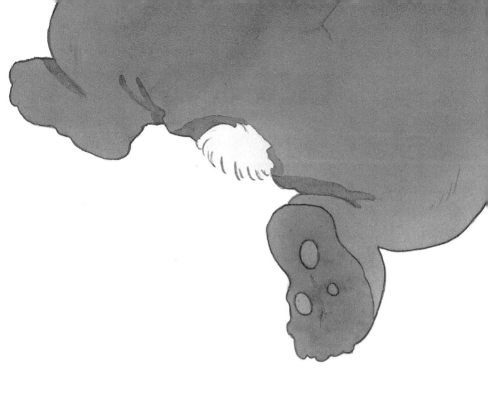

Big Bill growled reassuringly and disappeared. He was back in no time, and growled reassuringly again.

The next moment, powerful
hindquarters came over the edge of the
pit. And then the strange giant bear was
standing beside Old Mahony! He grabbed
the old man and lifted him up, as if he
were as light as a sack of feathers.

Big Bill held his paws out to the strange bear. The mother bear, the grandfather, and the bear cubs all held on to Big Bill's back legs, so that he didn't slide into the pit. But it was not so easy. The bears all had to heave and tug until at last they got the giant out, with Old Mahony in his arms.

The giant bear carefully set the old man down on the ground.

"Thank you," said Old Mahony quietly.

The darkness began to fade, and a
morning mist crept over the river.

The bears stood looking down at Old
Mahony.

"I'm sorry for everything!" said Old
Mahony. "And I'm glad you're all here—
especially since it took the whole family
to rescue me."

The bears grinned, and Big Bill thumped the old man affectionately on the shoulders.

Later they all ran down to the river and went swimming. Even Old Mahony jumped into the water. The old man splashed around and laughed happily. Having a family is fun, he thought.

Then Old Mahony and Big Bill showed
the others how to fish quietly in the river.

They all stood there, Old Mahony and
the Bear Family, fishing together, each in
his own way.

Wolfram Hänel was born in Fulda, Germany. He trained to teach English and German, but he decided not to go into teaching. Instead, he began to write plays and stories for children. Among his books for North-South are *Abby*, *The Other Side of the Bridge*, *Lila's Little Dinosaur*, *Mia the Beach Cat*, and the first book about Old Mahony and Big Bill, *The Old Man and the Bear*. He has two homes: one in Hannover, Germany, and one in Kilnarovanagh, a small village in Ireland, where there are no bears, but there is a river with big salmon in it.

Jean-Pierre Corderoc'h was born in Nantes, France. He studied art at the Ecole des Arts Décoratifs in Strasbourg. He has illustrated many children's books, including *The Old Man and the Bear*. He and his wife, who is also a picture book illustrator, and their two sons live in a two-hundred-year-old converted farmhouse in Brittany.